CW01468593

Amazon Kindle /KDP edition
Copyright 2023 – Ashley Todd

For Mick and Mark
For continuing to believe in me.

For Dan – for helping me create Frank and Astrid

Introduction

Choose Federal law enforcement.

Choose the military.

Choose NASA (National Aeronautical Space Administration) or the CDC (Centre for Disease Control).

Choose lying to your superiors.

Choose to ruin your career.

Choose to have no friends.

Choose divorce.

Choose viewing life through the bottom of a bottle.

Choose destroying evidence and executing innocent people just because they know too fucking much.

Choose black fatigues and matching gas masks.

Choose an Heckler & Koch MP5 stolen from the CIA (Central Intelligence Agency) loaded with lasers, with a wide range of fucking attachments.

Choose blazing away at mind-numbing, sanity-crushing targets from beyond the stars.

Choose to wonder if you would be better off stuffing the barrel in your own mouth.

Choose a 9mm retirement plan.

Choose going out with a bang at the end of it all.

Choose to have PGP-encrypting your last message down a securely laid cable as an NRO Enigma Wet Works squad busts through your door.

Choose one last night at the Opera.

Choose *Enigma Division*

N.B.

You do not choose Enigma Division; it chooses you.

It was late. Once again Astrid Baxter had been working after hours in her office. She pushed her glasses on to the top of her head, rubbed her eyes and stifled a yawn. The program still wasn't finished, though to be fair it could wait another day or so. The customer wasn't expecting it until the next week. She drained the last of the whiskey from her glass and pressed 'Save' on the computer keyboard.

The sound of *Pet Shop Boys* "West End Girls" filled the room as her cell phone started to ring. She picked it up, idly noticing that it was an unknown number.

"Hello, Astrid Baxter here, who is calling?" She asked quizzically. In her line of work as a computer consultant she was used to receiving phone calls from prospective customers at any time of the day.

A strange electronically generated voice spoke into her ear. "Astrid Baxter, Enigma Division requires your services. You are required to meet your partner Frank McLeod at the Post Office in New-Newbiggin tomorrow morning at 1030hours. You will use the phrase 'I hear the opera is coming' once you have identified him. His response will be 'I do love the theatre'. You will then liaise with your handler at the Post Office, who will provide you both with intel for your case. Do not discuss this with your family, or you will be punished. Failure to attend the meeting point and you will be punished. Failure to comply with the case and your entire family will be punished." The phone line went dead.

Astrid tossed the cell phone down on her desk, shaking as a long-suppressed panic began to set in. She took a deep breath as she opened the bottom drawer of her desk and pulled out the bottle of whiskey. She opened the lid and sloshed it into the glass till it was about half full. She gulped it down. She felt the whiskey burn against her throat.

Just who the hell were Enigma Division, and what did they want from her? She thought.

From where it lay on the desk, her cell phone beeped to indicate she had received a text message. Reluctantly, she picked it up. The message was again an unknown number, she opened the attachment with a sense of trepidation. What looked like a dossier appeared on her phone screen. It had a black cover and a glowing Division triangle, or Enigma symbol was on the first page.

Nervously, well aware that her life as she knew it would never be the same Astrid opened the document.

First was Intel regarding her partner for this mission; Francis (Frank) McLeod. Born: 1973 (now aged 44) in Glasgow Scotland. He joined the Scots Guard at the age of 16 and served four years before joining the SAS for 20 years. He now currently works as a freelance security contractor. Family: Nil. NoK (Next of Kin) Unknown.

"Well, what a load of B.S." Astrid muttered to herself, "Let's see what we can find out about you Frank."

Astrid opened up Google Chrome and carried out the usual searches for Francis (Frank) McLeod on social media: Facebook, Twitter, and LinkedIn.There was no trace of him. She tapped a biro against her teeth. Astrid then looked up private security contractors, again to very little avail.

"You slippery bugger Frank, where are you hiding, and more's the point why…?" she murmured.

Astrid's fingers danced across the computer keyboard and she opened a deep search engine. This allowed her to access the invisible web, the dark shady side of the internet that the public cannot access. Not only was Astrid a computer consultant who could strip and restore a computer in mere minutes, but she was also an esteemed computer hacker with less than legitimate skills.

This time when Astrid typed in McLeod's name she found a passport photograph taken, which given the age on his military records must have been taken around ten years ago. It showed a dark haired, cleanly shaven man with startling blue eyes and a sardonic smile on his face. "Well, well, well, now we know what you look like, let's see what else we can find out about you."

A few key taps later and Frank's military career in the Scots Guard was now onscreen, which included tours of Bosnia and Afghanistan. However, as expected, very little detail on his exploits in the SAS were available even on the invisible web, other than showing his rising to the rank of Captain, before leaving at the age of 40as a result of a voluntary discharge. But, other than that, there very little about the man himself, he was almost a ghost.

Astrid leant back in her chair and knocked back the rest of the whiskey in her glass, before pouring out another measure. She was tired, she glanced at her watch, it was almost 12.45am. She had one more task to complete before bed.

Astrid typed in the words 'Enigma + Division' into the search engine, only to be redirected through loop after loop. There are whispers of course, ghosts in the walls of the internet. Alien conspiracies. Men in Black. Cover ups.

"Hmmm, I wonder if the truth is stranger than fiction..." she muttered before finally closing down the computer. It was 1am, time for bed.

She drained the last of her glass, and placed both it and the remaining contents of the bottle of whiskey in the bottom drawer of her desk, before locking it with a small key which she then dropped inside the desk tidy, hidden in plain sight.

She walked along the corridor to her daughter Rachel's bedroom. She opened the door, and her heart was filled with pure love at the sight of the twelve year old tomboy bunched up in her duvet, snoring softly. Astrid silently walked over the bed and gently pushed her hair back from her face and kissed her forehead.

She then walked into her own bedroom, her husband David rolled over as she walked in. "Another late one Astrid?" As he yawned.

"Sorry, I think there's going to be a few more over the next few weeks." She said, as she changed into her night dress, she took off her earrings and placed them onto the bedside cabinet, beside her glasses before climbing into bed.

David put his hand on her thigh and started to slip it upwards.

"Not tonight Dave, it's late and I'm tired." She said rolling over onto her side.

"Fine." He huffed, a few minutes later; the gentle sound of his snoring again filled the room.

Astrid closed her eyes and started to settle down for sleep. As ever, her dreams were haunted by the memories of ten years ago. The acrid sour smell of captivity invaded her senses, of her and 19 others trapped in the bunker together, for three months without seeing, or even receiving any news from her family. Tears ran freely down Astrid's cheeks as she slept. The haunting continued; the sound of gunfire and the metallic smell of death she bore witness to, when one of her fellow captives was shot to smithereens. Another of the captives was so hysterical that the soldier, dressed entirely in black with his face covered, head-butted her to knock her out and silence her.

Then it was Astrid's turn, when she was picked up by another soldier, who carried her out from the bunker and into the daylight, that she truly believed that she would never see again. The brightness that day was blinding, almost unbearable. She almost begged for the darkness to end the pain in her eyes.

"Rachel do you want eggs with that?" Astrid asked her daughter the following morning as she poured out a glass of orange juice.

"No Mom, I need to shoot off. I have to recheck my assignment." Replied the dark haired girl who at a first glance could be mistaken as Astrid's twin.

"Didn't you check it last night? Why didn't you say anything?" Astrid asked with a shred of irritation in her voice.

"You were busy, and I didn't want to bother you." Rachel replied taking a last bite of her toast before gulping down the last of her juice. "Okay, I'm away, love you Mom… love you Dad." Rachel then picked up her rucksack and ran out of the door.

David looked up from his newspaper, "Are you home today or elsewhere?" he asked.

"Home most of today, I do need to go out for an hour or so this morning but that should be me," replied Astrid. Their eyes not meeting as she busied herself by collecting the dishes from the dining table.

David watched her for a second, trying to work out when this distance had entered their relationship, it was before Pablo the pool guy he was sure of it, although from what he could gather, that seemed to have fizzled out. He let out an inaudible sigh, "Okay then, I'll see you tonight at dinner." He stood up, grabbed his car keys. He then gave Astrid an awkward kiss on the cheek as he left the house.

Astrid poured out another mug of coffee from the percolator, she liked it strong and black. She sat down at the dining table. She looked over at the clock on the wall, it was just after 8am, two and a half hours to go until 1030hrs, when she would be meeting Frank. She wondered if he would resemble his photo she had found late last night. Her mind came back to the moment; coffee, that's what she needed right now to settle her nerves; as the bottle of whiskey that was locked in her desk drawer was not socially acceptable at 8am, especially with what lay ahead.

It would take an hour to reach the Post Office in the early morning Seattle traffic. The drive to New-Newbiggin was uneventful; the journey was assisted by repeated renditions of The Pet Shop Boys Greatest Hits.

She pulled her white Honda Civic into the car park situated around the corner from the Post Office, and climbed out. She still had half an hour to go before she was meant to meet the elusive Frank, so she decided to check out the area. To familiarize herself with escape routes, just in case.

New Newbiggin was a typical township in Seattle; not the most exclusive area, but not depraved either. People strolled down the sidewalk without any interaction towards one another, apparently oblivious to their surroundings, merely existing in their own private worlds.

One of Astrid's favorite past times as a child, and also as a young adult was people watching, trying to work out the back story behind people as they carried out their mundane every day tasks of life. She would create stories, including the escaped prisoner trying to fit in to the real world, blending in so he wouldn't be caught. Next, came the wholesome soccer mom, who went to every one of her childrens' games, yet at night time worked as a dominatrix in a seedy sex club with its own dungeon. Astrid smiled to herself, she had a very livid imagination and occasionally, very occasionally she would let it run amok. When she did, there were very few complaints from the recipient; as Pablo the pool guy could personally vouch. She let out a sigh of regret, last week she had fired him. He began to expect much more from their relationship, he expected her to leave David, even insinuating that David knew about them already. Of course, David knew, he always knew about her affairs; he just chose to ignore them. They were never discussed, but when her latest indiscretion was over she would drink, become maudlin then pull herself back together. It had been that way ever since... well, ever since she escaped. This desire to feel alive would take hold and she would act upon it, but once satisfied she always came back; always.

Astrid stood outside the Post Office, she read the small ads placed in the window. As she read the adverts for cots and kitchen wares she watched the reflections in the window pane.

She saw a man in the reflection. He was around six feet tall, dressed in a a long sleeved cream coloured t-shirt, dark combat trousers and military desert boots. His dark brown hair was longer than in the passport photograph, curling slightly due to the humidity, it was lightly peppered with grey. He looked like he hadn't shaven for a week and wasn't in any great hurry to start. He was broad shouldered and muscular, the cream top strained against his defined torso. This was a man who looked after himself and was clearly comfortable in his own skin.

Her eyes flicked from his reflection back to the small ads in the window.

"I hear the Opera is in town." She said, feigning interest in the advert for Patterdale Terrier puppies.

"Aye, I do like to watch." He replied with a broad Scottish accent that even though she had read his file managed to surprise her. "Baxter I presume?" he said with a wry smile.

"McLeod?" she replied mirroring the smile.

"Good to see you lassie," he said, glancing at his watch. "I believe we have a little time, and I dinnae ken about you but I'm starving. Let's gan have a brew."

Astrid finally turned and looked at him, she had a confused look on her face as if he were speaking a foreign language.

"Come with me, we'll have a cuppa." He translated with a sigh, striding across the road to Starbucks.

Astrid tutted to herself and followed after him. The pair walked inside to find it was almost empty, but for the barista cleaning the work tops with a damp cloth there was only a scattering of patrons.

Frank ordered an Earl Grey tea, and an espresso that Astrid had asked for. They then sat down in a booth and watched the world pass by in an amicable silence. Fifteen minutes to go...

"So lassie, did you get the phone call yesterday." Enquired Frank gently blowing at the steam rising from his tea cup.

Astrid took a sip of her hot bitter coffee, she nodded in reply. "Have you dealt with them before?" she asked.

Frank nodded casually running his right hand over the stubble on his chin. "Aye lass, many a time... This is your first time, I know, I've read your file. The best advice that I can give is do as they say, dinnae give them any chance to... Well, just do as they ask." He replied.

"Come on lass; let's get this over with..." Frank stood up and winked at the cute young barista that had served him. He walked out from the coffee shop, Astrid grabbed her bag and followed him.

Inside of the Post Office was pretty much what one would expect to see in an olde world post office from prohibition America; with counters and glass screens, sectioned into three areas; enquiries, deliveries and collections.

A portly old man with a kindly face sat behind the counter marked collections. He glanced up at Frank from his copy of the Times newspaper, and gave an almost invisible nod of acknowledgement in his general direction.

Frank approached his desk. "Aye sir, I'm here to pick up a package for McLeod and Baxter." He said with an air of arrogant authority.

The teller broke into a smile of recognition, "Fantastic, Mr McLeod, if you would like to sign here then I can get it for you." He handed Frank a sheet of creamy linen embossed paper, with a Division triangle printed in the top right hand corner. Frank traced the outline of the triangle briefly with his index finger, before using the silver pen that was chained to the desk to scrawl his name across the page. "And the lady too please." The teller said, looking at Astrid expectantly.

Astrid walked over and signed the document.

"Good day to you both, here is your package. I imagine that you are both in a hurry. Farewell." He said returning his attention to his newspaper.

"Ha'way Baxter, we have work to do." Said Frank, as he picked up the large manila envelope and headed out the door. Astrid looked back at the teller who flashed her smile, before running after Frank.

Around the corner from the post office, a 2017 Landrover Discovery in black was parked up, Frank opened the driver side door. "Hop in and let's take a look," he said.

"My parents always warned me about getting into cars with strange men," began Astrid, in an attempt to alleviate the mood.

"Good job you read my file then," said Frank, trying to hide his smile.

Astrid grinned as climbed into the car. "Let's see what Santa brought us then."

Frank placed the manila envelope on the dashboard. There was nothing written on it, save for a Division triangle printed on the right hand corner.

"I hope you're ready for your life to change forever Astrid. Once they have you in their clutches you can't ever walk away. Enigma will call when they want you, and if you want *them,* well they have the ability to stay well hidden in the shadows." He paused. "Let's see what the future holds for us."

Frank tore the envelope open, and shook the contents out onto the dashboard. Two iPhone 7's, a dossier marked *Eyes Only,* and a single key.

Frank opened the dossier up for both he and Astrid to read through.

Summary of a report on Clyde Baughman:

DOB: 03/28/1945
FAMILY: Wife, Marlene (08/20/1940-11/02/2002)
            Daughter, Sharon (09/12/1967)
            Son, Michael (07/28/1974)
OCCUPATION: Bureau of Internal Revenue (later IRS) (06/11/1965 – 09/01/1999) ret'd as Assistant Deputy Commissionaire for Operational Support.
Active with group from 1967 – 1970, taking part in 11 operations (details unavailable). Numerous consultations with a speciality in taxation and property confiscations. No current associations with the group.

The key upon examination was a standard front door key, and at this time didn't require any further scrutiny.

"I wonder…" began Astrid. But before she could continue one of the iPhones on the dashboard rang. She looked at Frank who nodded with suggestion for her to answer.
She picked up the phone.

"Hello?" she said warily, hitting the loudspeaker button so Frank could hear the other end of the conversation.

The electronically generated voice, similar to that from last night carried over the speaker. "Astrid Baxter, confirm your status."

Astrid looked over at Frank, a look of panic on her face; "We, erm, we have collected the package, and we're reviewing the contents."

The synthisised voice continued. "This is a salvage operation... you and Agent McLeod are required to go to the coordinates which will be sent to your phones in due course, once there you need to clear the area of any Intel which may be traced back to Enigma Division. Anything of a suspicious nature must be returned to the handler... You will find him at the Post Office. You have 48 hours to complete your mission. Failure to comply *or* to complete the mission will result in punitive action against both yourselves and your significant others. Is this understood?"

"Understood." Echoed Astrid, the colour draining from her face. The extent of her predicament was becoming all to real.

The phone went dead. Seconds later an incoming message bleeped on the screen. Frank opened the message to reveal some co-ordinates sent presumably from Enigma Division. He punched them into the Land Rover's Sat Nav system and a map showing the destination appeared on the screen.

"It's around a two hour drive, are you okay to follow in your little number?" Frank asked.

"Don't diss the ride Frank, she may be small but she is feisty." Replied Astrid, climbing out from the Land Rover.

"That's exactly what I'm afraid of..." muttered Frank as he watched her walk over to her little red Honda Civic, noting just how tightly her blue denim jeans hugged her backside. *She must workout regularly,* he thought.

Frank rubbed a hand over his face, "seriously get a god-damned grip, she's married, has a child, you're partners, the last thing you should be thinking about is that. But damn, she's one fine looking woman."

A car horn interrupted his less than pure thoughts as Astrid pulled up beside him, he wound the window down. "Follow at least two cars length behind, that was you keep me in sight, but it won't too obvious to anyone else, oh and take this, just in case." He passed Astrid one of the iPhones.

Frank drove on ahead. Astrid did as she had been instructed and followed Frank onto the freeway maintaining a strict two cars length behind him. She still drove with the dulcet tones of The Pet Shop Boys in her car. She tried to process what was going on and work out, and just how she had come to be contacted by Enigma Division in the first place.

Three weeks previously...

Flicking on the laptop, something didn't seem right. She couldn't place it at first, everything looked exactly as she had left it yet something was amiss.

Astrid looked closer at the desktop screen.

A sense of unease prickled at the back of her neck.

She opened the start screen and glanced through the documents and their order on the screen.

It was then that she saw it.

A working document entitled *Architect* that she had been working on it late the previous night. However, when she closed the document down she removed it the shortcut icon from the screen. It was also password protected with a randomised pin sentry. She clicked on the properties to check the last time that the file had been accessed and edited. The result showed it was accessed only two hours earlier.

"Bastards," she exclaimed.

She opened the folder with an increasing sense of fear. This folder contained her deepest thoughts and musings. She typed in her PIN and opened the file.

An entire page had been *added* to the file.

We are watching.
We are listening.
You will be contacted soon.Astrid Baxter, tell no one.
Trust no one.
Δ

She bit back the fear that filled her to the core, deleting the page as she did. She then reached into the bottom drawer of her desk and pulled out the bottle of Jack Daniels and poured out a generous measure into a glass before knocking it back. She continued to drink until she fell asleep at her desk, her head on her arms, reluctant tears flowing staining her blouse.

When she woke the following morning, she had a hangover from hell. She could remember nothing from the previous night.

Present Day - 14.45 Downtown Seattle, Baughman Residence

After two hours of travelling, the Landrover pulled up outside of an apartment block. The building itself was stark and ordinary. A basic ten storey block built from concrete bricks circa the 1970's when it would have been seen as innovative. Now, in 2017, it looked dark, desolate and depressing.

A man sat in the doorway with a brown paper bag swigging the hidden contents back. His eyes were dead, lifeless, having taken to viewing the world through that bottle and many more that preceded it. Astrid tried to hide the fear that she had met her future here. She and Frank walked into the lobby. It was shabby, paint peeled from the damp walls. The floor was uncharacteristically clean but was old and in desparate need of repair, much like the rest of the building. They walked to the elevator, the car was cold and cramped. A faint aroma of urine permeated within the confined space. Astrid gave an involuntary shudder as though someone had walked across her grave as she watched Frank punch the button for the third floor.

A sense of déjà vu overwhelmed her, and she felt the sting of as yet unshed tears fill her eyes. She pressed the heels of her hands against her eyes and took a deep breath to regain her composure.

Frank observed Astrid with great interest. She stood at around 5foot 2inches, dwarfed by his 6' 4" frame. Again, he admired her, dressed in those tight fitting blue jeans, brown cowboy boots, plaid shirt over a plain white t-shirt, and a brown leather vintage jacket. Her hair was sandy brown, tied back into a practical ponytail with a brown elastic band. Her bangs however, were falling out and they framed her face perfectly, making her look much younger than her 36 years would suggest. Her glasses were wire framed, again practical but they suited her, making her Division eyes seem bigger and more doe like. She wore a little too much makeup for his personal taste, but he could still appreciate her natural beauty. She was curved in exactly what Frank would call *all the right places*, her waist was trim, and she had what appeared to be a firm and well-rounded backside in those tight jeans.

He noticed her visible distress and was just about to press her as to why when the elevator stopped, they had reached the third floor. Astrid practically ran from the elevator when the doors opened.

The corridor was empty, with eight apartment doors; the floor had an ancient red runner that was frayed in places. The floorboards were stained dark with grime. The walls had woodchip paper that had been painted and repainted multiple times, on top of which it was stained with both nicotine from the aroma which hung so heavily in the air, and years of people running their hands along the surface of the walls.

A feeling of familiarity flowed through Frank, this place reminded him of the block of flats that he called home in Glasgow during his formative years. He was forever thankful that he no longer had to live in such conditions. He liked the minimalistic life, but also liked some luxuries that he worked hard to achieve in the years since he existed in such squalor.

They passed along the hallway, checking the doors as the went. The third door on the right hand side read number 38 in the grime of the door. The numbers had long since fallen from the door, but were still embossed in the filth.

Astrid looked at the keyhole, it was of the design that the key from the dossier should fit. She fished the key from her purse, cautiously glancing up and down the corridor before putting it in the keyhole. The key turned with little resistance, suggesting that the lock was well maintained.

She pushed at the door and it scraped across a small pile of mail that had been pushed through the letter box. She bent down to pick up the letters. Frank shamelessly took this opportunity to enjoy the sight of her peachy butt in those tight jeans...

"Instead of just standing there looking at my ass Frank, why don't you hold the door, or help me out?" Said Astrid, as she looked over her shoulder at Frank. She had to bite the inside of her cheeks, because as terrified as she was, Frank's barely concealed appreciation helped her keep the fear at bay.

"Hey, I'm only human Baxter, and if you bend over like that right in front of me, then you can't expect me *not* to look." He said as he chuckled, his eyes crinkling at the corners. Just for a fleeting moment, Astrid glimpsed the man behind the soldier, a man probably with a devilishly wicked sense of humour, and an eye of appretiation

Astrid glanced through the mail in her hands, it consisted mainly of junk mail, mail order catalogues mostly for model magazines, Airfix kits of military aircraft circa WW2. Nothing appeared to be out of the ordinary.

They walked further into the apartment, and Frank closed the door behind them. The apartment itself was small, very small. It consisted of a living room, a kitchen and dining area, bathroom with a shower and one double bedroom. The smell of nicotine permeated through each room, and the once white walls now had the yellow tinge, evidence of being the home of a heavy smoker.

At the right-hand side of the door there was a sideboard made of dark oak, in a glass dish on the top was a bunch of keys with numerous plastic tags attached, all of different colours. Frank picked them up from the dish and took a closer look at them; they were labelled: *Basement, Outhouse, Shed*, and *Septic Tank*. Baughman clearly had access to another building, Frank conclude. He placed them in his pocket, keen to pursue this angle later if the opportunity arised. This however, meant that the initial search might be more difficult than first anticipated if it involved more than one location.

Astrid walked into the living room. An old cracked brown leather two seater sofa, that looked like it should have stayed in the seventies where it hailed from engulfed the room. Opposite this was an old grey analogue television with a large back from the 1990s. A glass coffee table placed directly between the two. A somewhat poignant crossword puzzle that would-forever remain unfinished lay on the coffee table, with a black bic biro with a chewed lid resting on top of it.

A chipped mug, stained dark brown from black tea, sat on the table next to a box of sugar coated doughnuts which had gone dry and started to crumble to dust.

Frank picked up a doughnut and sniffed it curiously. Astrid looked over at him, and raised an eyebrow, a look of disgust on her face. "Seriously Frank, you are gross."

He chuckled, and reluctantly placed the doughnut back inside the box. He was planning on taking a bite. "Bloody women…." He muttered intentionally loud enough for Astrid to hear as he walked into the kitchen.

The kitchen again was sparse, but functional. It clearly belonged to an old man who rarely received visitors. There were two pans in the sink which had a weird fungus growing on them, but then it had been a week since the poor old guy had passed away.

Frank opened the fridge door, revealing it to be almost empty. A plate had a discoloured pack of open bacon on it, the milk had turned to cottage cheese, and a half lemon lay mummified on a shelf. It could almost be his fridge at home.

As he closed the fridge door a piece of paper became unstuck from the magnets and fell to the floor. He knelt down and picked it up.A crudely drawn stick man in wax crayon with a sun in the right-hand corner, a slash of Division 'grass' and a slash of blue 'sky' dominated the bottom and top of the page. A child's writing had entitled the picture 'Grandpa', and it was signed by 'Cassie,' and had earned her two gold stars, presumably awarded by her teacher.

Frank sadly placed the picture back on the fridge door, wondering how Cassie took the news that her Grandpa passed away.

Down the corridor Astrid had already opened the linen closet, it was filled with surprisingly amount of linen, although all of it with a slightly damp aroma. A couple of moths escape after Astrid rifled through the contents. She then closed the door, and slowly made her way to the bathroom.

The bathroom was a mess. The towel rack had been pulled from the wall and lay twisted on the floor. The shower door was cracked, the bath had what looked like a rust stain from a shower attachment. The stench of death lingered.

"Christ this is where he died, poor bastard," Astrid said, as she opened the medicine cabinet to check through the contents.

There was a half empty tube of Polygrip, a bottle of Pepto-Bismol, a single Division toothbrush, and a bottle of aspirin in the cabinet. Astrid took another sad glance around the place of Baughman's demise before walking out and closing the door behind her.

Only one room remained to be looked through, the bedroom. Astrid took a deep breath and walked inside, Frank was already sat on the bed reading through a pile of paperwork. He looked up at her and nodded over towards the desk in the corner of the room.

On the desk there was a laptop, a bog standard generic laptop of around five years old, it was plugged into the mains socket, and the Division light indicated a full charge.

"I saw that and thought I'd best leave it for the IT lass. There's some interesting stuff here though. Baughman had a cabin in the sticks, about an hour's drive from here, I thought we might check it out once we are done here?"

Astrid nodded non-committedly as she approached the desk.

Beside the laptop, there was an old photograph of Clyde Baughman and his wife Marlene in an old gilded silver frame. Astrid picked it up for a closer look, and the uneasy feeling raised its ugly head once more.

What at a first glance looked like a lovely photograph, rapidly became tainted upon closer examination. The couple stood in front of a lake on what looked like Memorial Day weekend judging by the decorations in the background.

However the once beautiful photograph had since been marred by the barbaric etching out of Marlene's eyes with either a pencil or pen, so the point where only two large X's now resided where her eyes should have been. This made Astrid feel eerily uncomfortable.

"Frank, what do you make of this?" Astrid asked, unable to hide the unease and fear in her voice.

Frank placed the pile of paperwork on the bed beside where he sat. He stood up and walked over to the desk, he took the picture frame from Astrid's hands and looked closely at the photograph. He reflexively rubbed his right hand across his jaw as he tried to process the image in front of him.

"Christ Astrid, this is some seriously fucked up shit," he said. "Scratching out eyes, that's kind of anti-possession, if the eyes aren't there then they cannot see you, or see what's going on. The poor guy must have been driven mad; trying to dehumanise, and distance himself from his wife, that's dark deep shit. I guess we can take it as evidence for Enigma, it's definitely high on the weird shit-o-meter."

He replaced the frame on the desk and wiped his hands on his combat trousers almost as though they were tainted by whatever had haunted Baughman's psyche.

The other photographs on the table included a graduation photographs of Clyde and Marlene's daughter Sharon and son Michael and a photograph of a blonde haired child with chocolate covering her face. Which was sat in pride of place beside a paperweight with a child's handprint with the inscription 'Cassie age four' written on it. Astrid presumed this was a teacher's handwriting as it was far too advanced for a four-year-old.

Astrid smiled as she had a similar one on her desk at home with Rachel's handprint from kindergarten.

"Are you actually going to look at the laptop Astrid or are you aiming to just increase the suspense here?" teased Frank.

"Sorry, just trying to get a feel for things…" apologised Astrid, before she noticed the smile from Frank, and realising it was sarcasm she winked back.

Cracking her knuckles, she opened the laptop and booted it up. The start-up screen cycled through, and Astrid noticed that the laptop was so old it still ran on windows XP.

She smiled to herself "Child's play…"

A password prompt appeared on the screen; "At least he was security conscientious I suppose" she said to herself.

Astrid now had two options; she could bust into the computer using her 'specialised skills' but where was the challenge in that? Or, she could try and figure out the password.

She glanced back at Frank who was waiting expectantly sat on the bed. Her answer of course, was to find the password. A need to prove herself against this ex soldier raised its ugly head.

"Problem?" asked Frank, leaning forward with curiosity.

"Not at all, just trying to guess a password. It's locked" she replied motioning to her laptop.

"You can't tell me you can't get into the thing... you're supposed to be well versed in that field, c'mon, bust the little bastard open."

Astrid stifled a laugh, "I'm on it, just trying to use a front door key rather than C4, okay?.. Hmmm I wonder..." she typed in the name *Cassie*. A box appeared on the screen: Incorrect password. She chewed her lip and looked at the desk, "aged four huh..."

Again she typed in Cassie, but added 2013, being Cassie's year of birth. "Booyah!" she shouted as the desktop opened.

Frank came over and stood at the side of her as she sat on the chair at the desk and started to flick through the folders.

"Christ, Astrid - remind me to clear my browser history before letting you anywhere near my laptop," he muttered, as he watched her flick through page after page.

"Even if you did Frank, there's still a trail!" She replied, watching for his reaction in the reflection of the laptop screen.

"Really? Awww fuck!" he groaned, then grinned sheepishly, "Ahh well, there's a canny porn stash on there anyway, and I can always let it be my legacy. Right Baxter, what else have we got here then? Any thing else jumping out."

As Astrid searched, a file caught her eye, or rather didn't catch her eye. A hidden file, albeit crudely hidden, consisting of an entire folder. An invisible folder on the desktop.

"What the hell is that?" asked Frank leaning in closer.

Astrid could feel his warm breath tickling against her ear, the musky smell of his aftershave evaded her senses, she felt her heart skip a beat, was it being so close to what could only be described as a raw, masculine man, or what is the task at hand?. She let out a slow even breath as she clicked on the folder.

Again, a password prompt came on the screen, however this time it carried an extra warning.

No unauthorised access.
Three attempts only!
 Failed entry will result in the files will be completely destroyed beyond repair.

"Fuck, a burn-drive. I need to get this right." She murmured.

Again, Astrid glanced around looking the bedroom looking for inspiration. The photograph of Clyde and Marlene struck a chord. She looked at the photograph and the frame for a second, then she turned it over and opened the back of the frame. Written on the back were the words 'Lake Tahoe, 1978'.

Astrid chewed her lip for a moment, considering her options, "Fuck it, I'm going to try this."

Astrid took a deep breath, held it and typed in the words 'lake tahoe 1978', time seemed to slow to a halt. Astrid was acutely conscious of every beat of her pulse, the air seemed to become still as the computer in front of her ran her password.

A giant X appeared on the screen, Astrid swallowed back the bilious taste that filled her mouth, her palms began to sweat and she felt the colour drain from her face.

"Its okay Baxter, you have two more tries." Said Frank, trying to hide the frustration in his voice, he wasn't however, very successful.

Astrid shot him a glance, "I was sure I had it... Ooh, case sensitive! You bastard! Come on!"

Again Astrid typed in the words 'Lake Tahoe 1978' ensuring that she used uppercase letters as appropriate this time. She didn't realise that she was holding her breath again, until the file opened.

"You fucking genius!" said Frank with a laugh.

Once opened, the folder was seen to be full of photographs, hundreds of photographs of what looked like ancient text, written in a foreign language, an ancient language, that possibly looked like Latin. It contained aged pages, written in ornate ancient text, with sketches of people filled the folder. Each photograph had the eyes of the people shown scratched out.

"What the hell? What kind of crazy shit were you into Clyde?" asked Frank as he looked at the computer screen. Astrid's hand plugging something into the USB port caught his eye.

"What the hell do you think you are doing Baxter?" as he registered the flash drive. Astrid quickly selected all the files and transferred them to the drive.

"Let's call it insurance," she replied, unplugging the drive, capping the end and slipping it inside her t-shirt, and into her bra. She looked at Frank defiantly, daring him to challenge her.

"It's your funeral Baxter…" he said, shrugging his shoulders, but again a feeling of foreboding trickled down his spine. "Well I guess we should contact our handler and let them know what we've found."

Frank pulled out his iPhone. He flicked open the unlock screen and pressed the Division Enigma icon on the home screen. The familiar robotic voice came over the loud speaker. "Report."

"We have recce'd the address. Intel has been collected, a laptop with images and text, photographs. There is also a secondary location – a cabin." Replied Frank.

"You have a new objective… Investigate the cabin. Drop the materials at the Post Office at 0900 hours tomorrow. Search the cabin for offending and material of interest, gather the information together and send to Enigma. Remember, time is of the essence." The phone line went dead.

Astrid looked at Frank, "Let's get this stuff together and get away from this place, it creeps me out." She placed the laptop inside a laptop bag that she found on the floor beside the desk, and picked up the defaced photograph. Frank added the paperwork relating to the cabin to the pile.

As they exited the apartment and Astrid locked the front door, the apartment door opposite opened.

"Shit, think of something quick!" muttered Frank, as an elderly woman stepped out the door with a small Bichon Frise on a pink sparkly leash.

"So, Mr Chapman, I do hope that you find the apartment to your liking, as I said it's a great location," said Astrid desperately hoping that they would get away with this. "Oh, and here we have one of your possible new neighbours, Ms…"

"Mrs Janowitz," replied the old woman, looking a little confused. "The place isn't up for sale already? The poor man hasn't even been buried. For shame."

She shook her head in disgust.

"Mrs Janowitz, I do apologise, it must seem so callous, but we have had a lot of interest in this location, and well this gentleman was keen to have a look as soon as we could arrange it." Replied Astrid, crossing her fingers behind her back.

"That poor, poor man. He was never the same after his wife passed away. He locked himself away from the world afterward it happened. Did you know it was three days before they found him? So very sad." Mrs Janowitz locked her front door and proceeded to the end of the corridor with the little white dog trailing behind her, headed for the staircase.

As she left, Frank looked over to Astrid, "Good save, but after that I'm not buying the place, let's get away from here, and fast."

Astrid nodded in agreement and the pair briskly strolled into the elevator. Frank punched the ground floor button and the elevator rumbled back to life.

As they left the apartment block, the old man was still sitting in the doorway, his eyes a little glassier than before. Frank pressed a twenty dollars bill into his hand.

"Go and get something to eat mate," He urged kindly.

He looked over to Astrid and shrugged his shoulders. "People chose to forget for so many reasons, that's their choice but they still need to continue the basics. I'm not naive enough to think he'll spend it on food, but at least for a few moments he will believe that someone gives a shit."

This humanitarian gesture surprised Astrid, she was noticeably warming to Frank.

The two walked back towards their respective cars, Frank shook his head. "Nope, get in mine, its sturdier, we don't know what the roads are like towards the cabin. Yours will be... fine here."

Astrid rolled her eyes. She abandoned getting in her Civic, she walked around the passenger side and jumped inside Frank's Landrover. She fastened her seat belt as Frank typed in the location of the cabin into the satnav. He then started the engine and started to drive out from the parking lot, and the beautiful yet haunting voice of Annie Lennox filled the car, 'Sweet Dreams are made of these, who am I to disagree...'.

"Scotland has three great exports as far as I am concerned;" began Frank with a smile. "Irn Bru – which is orange coloured nectar, Annie Lennox and also Susan Boyle. Now, there's two women with amazing voices, I dinnae care what Simon Cowell has planned for her these days, but crikey I'm convinced that crazy lass fell from the sky because her voice is heaven sent. Of course we have also exports like two A-MAZ-ING Doctor Who's, and John Barrowman you lucky buggers. Mind all the time I've been here I still miss Greggs, never found anything like it."

"What on earth is Greggs? Seriously Frank it's like you speak a foreign language."

Frank slammed the brakes on causing the car to screech to a halt. Astrid shot forward in her seat. Frank's body shook with laughter.

"Bloody hell Astrid, you crack me up lass. Greggs is one of the most delicious pastry based product bakers from the North East of England, also home to a rubbish football team and a not so rubbish one."

He started to drive again holding up his hand in a wave of apology to the cars behind him. Astrid was left lost for words at this rugged Scotsman, who she couldn't help be drawn to, he had a wicked tongue in cheek sense of humour which radiated from him, yet a shadow of darkness lurked in the sidelines, it had to, otherwise he wouldn't be working for Enigma Division. She yearned to discover his dark side.

It was another long drive to the cabin. Astrid was happy to be able to relax. She leaned back in the seat and listened to the beautiful voice of Annie.

18.05 The Cabin (in the woods)

Frank turned down into what looked like a private road, loose stone and hardcore covered the otherwise muddy surface. Astrid was quietly thankful that she was in the Landrover rather than her little Civic, the suspension would not have survived the journey otherwise.

Either side of the track there were dense trees that fed into Beacon Food Forest. The little beaten track led almost to the door of an isolated, and dilapidated looking log cabin. A large field stone chimney looked to provide the heat. To the left of the cabin there was an old well, presumably the water source for the cabin.

"Care to have an explore?" asked Frank, stopping the Landrover.

"Sure, why not?" Replied Astrid, unbuckling her seat belt and climbing out of the car.

Frank opened the boot of the car and took out a bag he looked through it and pulled out a gun which he stowed in his holster, he looked at Astrid, "Are you carrying?

Astrid looked terrified; she shook her head in reply. "I've never even held one."

Frank went back into the bag and pulled out a smaller gun, he loaded the clip with six rounds of ammunition, cocked it back then slid in the clip. "This is a Walther PPK, same as James Bond and Peggy Carter carry, when the slide is back like this it cannot be fired, release the slide, [click] this way, to let you fire. Spread your legs to balance your weight, hold with one hand and support with your other, then point and shoot. Got it? Here you go." He passed the gun to Astrid who gingerly placed it in her jeans pocket.

"Just in case, there's bears and shit round here. I just have a weird feeling about this place." Muttered Frank. "Come on then Baxter, let's get going."

They walked to the well which was covered with a large grid it was still connected and looking down they could see deep water at the bottom. Their reflections indicated just how deep the shaft went.

They walked around to the back of the cabin, which backed against the woodland. There was an outhouse there, and what looked like a storage shed. Astrid opened the outhouse door, it looked like it hadn't been used for sometime, and thankfully it was still clean, she closed the door. Whistling 'All Star" Frank looked over and raised an eyebrow.

"Get out of my swamp…" he growled, mimicking Shrek

Astrid sniggered understanding the reference, she then walked over to the shed.

"I'm going to try the cabin, keep the gun close and shout if you need me." Frank said as he strolled over to the rear of the cabin and tried the lock with the unmarked keys on the large bunch of keys that he had swiped earlier from the Baughman house. A key worked and the door opened easily. He glanced back over his shoulder to check Astrid was okay before heading inside.

Astrid inspected the shed, it was old and a little rickety much like everything else around here. It was also locked tight, again like it hadn't been used for some time, and she was just about to go ask for the keys from Frank when something else caught her eye.

A hatch protruded from the ground, next to the septic tank, which struck Astrid as a little strange. She walked over to it for a closer look. A septic tank would usually be buried, not exposed like this, and the earth was piled around the outside which suggested that it had been exposed in this manner for some time. The hatch was also chained and padlocked shut.

Astrid bit her lip, she wasn't an expert, but this didn't look right by any means. The handle and the hinge of the door were well maintained and oiled. She glanced back at the cabin, which now had lights on. She could see the silouette of Frank moving back and forth against the window, he was busy exploring the interior of the cabin.

She looked back at the tank, it didn't add up. The tank was too big for the needs of the cabin and its potential occupancy. She stamped down on the hatch, the sound echoed beneath her. She was just about to head back to the cabin and Frank when she heard a muffled cry. It came from beneath her, beneath the hatch. She froze in horror, again the cry carried up. She crouched down and pressed her ear to the hatch, she could hear a mewling, sobbing cry.

Horror filled her, memories of her own entrapment threatened to consume her.

She banged hard on the hatch, "I'm here, we'll get you out of there, just hold on!!"

She ran to the cabin screaming Franks name in terror "Frank, there's someone trapped. The tank, they're in the fucking tank! Help me!!"

Frank shot to the door, "What the hell are you talking about? Where?"

Astrid grabbed his arm and practically dragged him to the septic tank hatch. She was white as a sheet.

The sun had disappeared below the tree tops, it had started to get dark, and the temperature had instantly dropped a couple of degrees. Frank reached into his combat trousers and pulled out a compact Cree torch. He switched it on and the beam lit up on the septic tank door.

Astrid's entire body was shaking with terror; she banged on the hatch, "Hello! We are here… We'll get you out of there." She shouted at the hatch.

Frank pressed his ear to the hatch and listened, he looked back at Astrid, "Lassie there's nowt..." he began, then the faintest cry echoed through the hatch. He looked back at Astrid.

''Fucking hell… there *is* someone down there! You were right. Shit!" He got up and ran back to the Land Rover and opened the back door. He pulled his kit bag out and onto the ground, he opened it and pulled out a large gun, it was a Heckler & Koch MP5 sub machine gun, finshed in matte black for stealth and modified to hell. He also pulled out a rope which he slung over his shoulder, before striding back to the septic tank hatch to where Astrid still looked petrified.

He placed the gun and the coil of rope on the ground. He reached into his pocket and found the keys. He then placed the torch between his teeth as he checked through the tags till he found the one marked septic tank. He pushed the key into the lock and turned it with great ease in the lock. He pulled the lock off discarding it to one side. He then dragged the hatch door open.

They both peered down the shaft that stretched out beneath them. Below the tank was dark, as expected. Frank shone the torch down the hatch, there were no ladders, it was a vertical drop. He could see the torch beam terminate on the tank floor. He estimated a drop of around twelve feet. The base looked dark and slightly damp, with a shallow patches of water on the floor. Moving the torch back and forth he gauged the tank as around twelve feet wide and twenty feet long. There was no evidence to suggest that it had ever been used as a septic tank. The torch outlined what looked like a woman in the corner, crouched down hiding from the light. Her sobs echoed around the tank. The reality of the moment dawned on them both. They looked at each other, both knowing exactly what the other was thinking. How long had she been in there?

"We have to get her out!" begged Astrid tears streaming down her face.

"I know, we will. Aye lass, we're going to get you out. I'm coming down!" shouted Frank into the hatch.

The woman's cries grew louder and desparate, and all the more pitiful, "Help me, he trapped me down here!" She cried her voice hoarse with dehydration and lack of use.

Frank grabbed the rope and passed it around his waist, tying it firmly in a bowline knot. He fastened the other end to the hinge on the door. It looked strong enough to hold his 16 stone frame.

"Astrid I need you to shine the torch down for me so I can see what I'm doing, I also need you to guide me okay?"

Astrid nodded. Frank gave her brief instructions how to body-belay. He instructed her to lie down on the ground and let the rope travel over her shoulder and through her hands which at the same time that she would be holding the torch.

"Right lass, I trust you, I'm a heavy bloke though so I need you to be sure, okay." He asked.

"It's fine Frank, just help her, please."

Frank lowered himself over the edge, with Astrid's help taking the slack he was able to lower himself down with Astrid watching his every move, bracing herself against the weight of Frank and the rope rubbing across her shoulder blade, her leather jacket offered some protection against the rope chaffing against her skin.

"Almost there, what's your name?" he shouted into the darkness.

The dry cracked voice called out, "Marlene, my name is Marlene."

Astrid almost dropped the torch in shock, the rope slipped through her hands, burning them, she cried out in pain. Frank bellowed as he plummeted eight feet to the ground.

"What the fuck happened there, Astrid are you okay?" he shouted peering up through the shaft.

"I'm sorry Frank! Are you okay?" shouted Astrid shining the torch down.

"I'm okay don't worry," he said as he turned towards the woman in the corner. "Marlene, I'm here, I'm going to help you out of here, okay."

The woman was still crouched down, sobbing to herself.

"Marlene, I'm here, I'm coming towards you, don't worry, I'm here to help." He inched closer and closer splashing through the puddles on the floor. He stretched his arms out towards the crouched and terrified woman.

Her head turned toward him slowly, her grey hair was lank, it was damp through condensation and sweat, and hung in strings around her face. Patches were missing as though ripped out from her scalp, her hands were bloodied from scraping at the walls in vain efforts to clib up and reach the underside of the locked hatch. Her flesh was blue and bloated, her eyes tinged with blood, sunken deeply into her face.

She looked like a bloated corpse; the smell that oozed from her body was much like a bloated corpse too. The only difference being, that this bloated corpse still breathed.

Frank took a step back in horror.

"Help meeee!" She cackled, reaching her arms toward him. "Help me!"

Frank chewed back the bile that filled his throat from the pungently sweet smell of decaying flesh, and stepped back once more.

"Astrid, I want you to start pulling the rope back, slowly." He said in a calm voice, hiding the terror that filled him.

"I can't see have you got her?" shouted Astrid into the darkness.

"Just start pulling back." He ordered again in a level voice.

Astrid grasped at the rope with her injured hands, and pulled back with all her might, grimacing against the burning sensation in her palms.

"Noooo you can't leave! Not without me." Shrieked the wretched creature named Marlene. Her entire body whipped around and she hurtles towards Frank, grabbing at his body and clothing and pulling him down with superhuman force. Astrid cried out as the rope dragged through her hands burning them once more.

"I'm fucking leaving… and not with you." Frank reached into his cargo pants and pulled out his pistol. He shot at the creature that was Marlene. A double-tap. The bullets tore through her shoulder, it would've been enough to stop any normal person, and it should have been enough to stop her in her tracks but it didn't. She ripped at his body, catching his shoulder with her claw like hands. Pain raked through his shoulder like hot fire, his shout of pain echoed through the septic tank.

Astrid tried once again to pull him up, but he was too heavy, her hands too broken.

She felt helpless. Tears of despair streamed down her cheeks, she looked to her right hand side and saw the MP5 laying next to her. She grabbed at it and biting against the pain in her hands aimed through the sight at Marlene.

She pulled the trigger, bullets spewed out, with barely a sound, a click and a pop in quick succession, muffled by the state-of-the-art suppressor, all shots seemed to miss Marlene.

The creature whipped her head upwards and peered through the shaft. Her eyes met Astrid's, as terror filled her body. The creature Marlene seemed to set herself back on her haunches, momentarily braced herself, then pounced upwards.

Astrid slid backwards, away from the edge of the hatch. The creature landed outside the tank, exactly where Astrid had been lying, she snarled at Astrid, her eyes glowed.

"Bitch!" she spat at Astrid.

Astrid shuffled back lifting the MP5 again, she closed her eyes and pulled the trigger.

A bullet hit Marlene's torso again, ripping right through it. The creature looked down and made a sound eerily like laughter. "You think you can stop me, you putrid mewling quim."

Down in the septic tank Frank could hear the gunfire. He desperately tried to pull himself up using the rope that was still attached to the hatch hinge. His shoulder was bleeding profusely, the pain and burning sensation weakened him. He was helpless, but Astrid was on her own.

Above him, the creature inched closer and closer to Astrid, it was hissing and spitting at her. She fired again. This time the crucial shot missed its target. Again, Marlene cackled in response. She ran towards Astrid grabbing her by the shoulder and throwing her to the ground in one fluid move.

Astrid choked on her breath, winded by the impact on the ground, reflexively she kicked back at her as hard as she could. The kicked hit her square in the chest, which seemed to weaken her, or at the very least stun her.

Down in the septic tank, Frank used his belt to create a makeshift tourniquet on his arm, pulling it as tightly as he could. He could hear Astrid's screams of terror and the inhuman noises erupting from Marlene.

"Focus Frank, Fucking focus." He thought, grasping the rope with both hands, he kicked against the damp floor and swung towards the wall. Bracing his feet he started to climb upwards. His shoulder screamed with pain but it was nothing compared to the screams of terror he could hear above him. He fought back against the pain that burned through his entire body. His entire focus was in getting out of the shaft to help Astrid.

Astrid looked at Marlene in horror as this creature just kept coming at her. The MP5 was out of ammo, she was now unarmed. Then in an instant she remembered the Walther PPK in her pocket and pulled it out, she vaguely remembered Frank telling her she had six rounds, six attempts to get this monster away from her. Six chances, no more.

She squeezed the trigger and felt the slight recoil from the gun, it hit Marlene on her other shoulder and knocked her backwards. However, this only resulted in angering her further, Astrid fired again, this shot going wide of its target.

Frank bellowed "Astrid, get down!" and fired his hand gun with frightening accuracy from where he was hanging from the rope, just below ground level

Marlene roared in fury, she turned, then ran towards Frank. He had now cleared the hatch, he fired shot after shot, but he may have well been firing jelly beans for his low calibre sidearm had little effect on the tornado that headed towards him.

Marlene flew at Frank, wildly, hissing, spitting, and scratching in his direction. She whipped her hands across Frank's chest, ripping clean through his cream t-shirt, Frank felt yet another sear of pain, the warmth started to drain as the blood started to flow from the laceration in his chest. He stumbled back in pain, he stumbled, hitting the ground hard. From his prone position, he lifted the gun and continued shooting in Marlene's direction but the pain was so intense he could barely focus on holding the gun, let alone aim it with any accuracy.

Frank braced himself. This was it. His vanquisher was almost on top of him. He fired the last round, the slide on his pistol locked back. Defeated he put the gun down and closed his eyes ready to fall into the cold, dark abyss of death.

Astrid however, wasn't out of ammo, she ran over shooting wildly with the Walther PPK, the first two shots fired hit their target but had little effect as to wounding her, but served somewhat as a distraction.

The creature that was Marlene turned around to face Astrid once again and let out an other worldly shriek, fear coursed through Astrid's veins, Marlene again hurtled towards her screaming and shrieking, her movements were erratic, fast and yet calculated.

Astrid braced herself for the impact murmuring a silent prayer "Please God, look after Rachel, please, oh please..."

Time seemed to slow down. Tick...tock...tick...tock...

Marlene's screams grew more and more guttural and animalistic, then…nothing…..

Astrid opened her eyes to see the creature that was Marlene had run past her and had continued into the woods.

Frank lay on the ground, clutching at his torso. Astrid broke through the fear that threatened to engulf her, she ran over to Franks aid.

"Frank, can you hear me?" she asked forcefully. "Frank it's me its Astrid."

Frank's eyelids fluttered, "For fuck's sake Astrid, stop fucking yelling, go in the back of the Land Rover, under the driver's seat there's a first aid kit underneath, and bring it here will ya."

Astrid raced to the Land Rover and opened the drivers side rear door, as stated there was a first aid box in the seat well. Although it wasn't all that large, she grabbed it with both hands and ran back to Frank cradling it as if she were carrying a baby.

Frank had pulled apart the shredded remains of his t-shirt. He exposed the mangled lacerations that covered his broad muscular chest, the blood although still flowing had started to clot and matt into the dark hair that covered his torso.

Astrid opened the first aid kit and handed Frank a bottle of Betadine solution. "I think it's supposed to be diluted…" she began. "Nope, okay then.." she continued as he poured the neat solution directly onto the wounds., His face grimaced at the sting of the iodine on the open wound. He then ripped open a sterile pad open with his teeth and rubbed it against his wounds, dislodging the coagulated crust and making the blood flow freely. He then poured on more Betadine, then applied another sterile pad which he held in place as Astrid applied torn off lengths of surgical tape to keep it in place. In an instant blood started to reappear through the dressing. But there was nothing more either of them could do with the meagre supplies they had.

"Fucking bitch - where the hell did she go?" He asked reaching into the kit and pulling out a bottle of Codeine Phosphate. He shook six tiny tablets into his hand, and knocked them back, dry swallowing, he then pulled out a vial of Penicillin. Then after finding a suitable syringe, he drew it up and injected himself intramuscularly in the arm before bundling up the contents of the box.

"She ran off to the woods, Frank she was so fast… I thought we… I thought she… I thought you… Oh my God… what the fuck have we done?" Astrid ran her hands through her hair clutching at it is despair. A look of shock and disbelief on her face.

"Let a fucking crazy ass bitch zombie escape by the looks of it! Fucking hell Astrid, help me get back to the cabin. Before you called me out here I found a footlocker, it looked important.Let's see what's in it, then we are going to have to call this in, Enigma *will* need to know."

"I don't know what I am more afraid of." Replied Astrid, as she helped Frank up into a standing position.

Whilst still keeping hold of his arm, Astrid stepped under it and pulled Frank's arm across her shoulders to support him as he half walked, half staggered into the cabin. He was clearly in a lot of pain. A fine sheen of sweat now covered his face. He showed a vulnerability that she had not seen before. This made her somewhat attaracted to him.

They stepped inside the dank, dark cabin, walking through the living room, andthen into Baughman's bedroom. A Division military footlocker with the hinges busted open lay on the floor.

Astrid lowered Frank into a seated position on the bed, "I'm glad I opened the fucker beforehand." He muttered, rubbing his hand over his face, "sure as fucking hell couldn't do it now."

Astrid noticed that his eyes were slightly glassy and his speech although still lucid was slightly slower and on the verge of slurring, as the codeine had started to kick in.

Astrid kneeled down and started to flick through the contents of the footlocker, it contained mostly photographs of Clyde, Marlene and their children and granddaughter. There was also a number of VCR tapes with FBI evidence tags dated 15/08/72 – 29/09/72, equating to around 21 hours of footage. Finally Astrid found an envelope; she held it up. "Open it." instructed Frank. Her hands shook as she opened the envelope and started to read the contents.

"To Whom It May Concern, if you are reading this, I can assume that I have died or become incapacitated before I have the courage to complete my final mission. You will find about 20 gallons on gasoline in the shed behind the cabin. It needs to be poured into the septic tank behind the cabin and ignited. You'd be happier if you didn't look inside. Please make sure that the remains are kept away from my children. I am so sorry. God please forgive me."

The letter fell from her grip and fluttered to the floor from Astrid's fingertips. She pressed a hand to her mouth. "She's out, oh fuck Frank, what did I do? Oh god what have I done!" she said in horror as she slumped to the floor, broken.

"You didn't know Astrid, Ha'way lassie, we need to gather all this together, and I'll call it into Enigma." Frank stood up, and lurched forward. "Whoa, up a little too quickly there." He said, steadying himself.

Astrid gave herself a mental shake, wiping away the unfallen tears on the back of her hand. Once she regained her composure she gathered together the materials, placing them back inside a kit bag that was also inside the footlocker, which she then picked up and slung over her shoulder.

"Come on then Frank. Lets get you away from this hellhole." as she led the way from the cabin, once outside, she then had to wait for Frank to walk out before the locking the cabin door behind them.

She could hear him softly humming, then singing "The hills are bare now, And autumn leaves lie thick and still...Oh Flower of Scotland, when will we see your like again..."

"Are you stoned? Jesus Christ Frank exclaimed Astrid opening the rear door of the Land Rover; she placed the kitbag on the back seat. She then opened up the passenger side door and helped Frank to climb inside.

"I'm fine, I'm fine," he said wincing as he climbed inside and sat on the seat. "Let's get this over with and ring Enigma." He said with a relieved sigh.

Astrid picked up the iPhone and pressed the Enigma symbol, she placed the phone on loudspeaker. The robot voice came over the speaker. "Status report."

"There was a creature, it was hidden in the septic tank, it escaped. It was Marlene, Baughman's dead wife; she was possessed by some kind of monster. We shot her, but she escaped." Babbled Astrid.

"Repeat Agent Baxter, status report. Facts not supposition."

Astrid took a deep breath.

"The mission is compromised. Dangerous subject on the loose, escaped from the septic tank. I repeat *dangerous*. Baughman had a creature trapped in the tank, I believe it's his wife. It is travelling at high speeds, maybe believe back to Seattle. There is a link there with Baughman's family."

There was a silence on the phone as the information just handed over was digested.

"That's all understood. Agent Baxter and Agent McLeod your mission has now changed. All Intel is to be deposited with the handler at the Post Office at 13.00 hours tomorrow. You have until then to gather information which will allow you to track and destroy the creature. Utilise all of Agent McLeod's military skills. If you fail both of you will pay dearly."

The phone line went dead.

"Well then, let's haul ass back to Seattle, let's try and make some sense out of this mess."

Astrid started the engine. She had to drive as Frank was in no fit state, and reversed out from the driveway to the cabin. She drove down the narrow, winding country road. She took a quick glance over towards Frank, he looked pale, possibly slightly feverish. "Frank, do you need anything, we can stop en route?" she asked with genuine concern in her voice.

"I'm fine really, there's some water in my bag, I'll just have some of that. These painkillers have me jiggered. Are you okay to drive back to Seattle?" He reached back and pulled a bottle of water from the black rucksack. He opened the bottle and took a long drink, he then passed the bottle over to Astrid who gratefully took a swig.

"We need to get you back to yours, get you cleaned up and decide our next move." Began Astrid.

"When we get to mine, you can download those book pages, hopefully there will be something that will help us track down that creature. I need a shower, a drink and something to eat. You look like you could do with the same. Then we'll get our heads down for an hour or so, then tomorrow we tackle this, prepared, with fresh eyes."

With that, Frank switched on the car radio, The Pet Shop Boys filled the car with "West End Girls", Astrid hid a smile, but not before Frank caught it.

"You're bonny lass when you smile," he said softly. "That's not meant in any way to be pervy, now what's the joke?"

"This is my favourite song; it's even my ringtone on my phone." She replied, a hint of pink colouring her cheeks.

Frank chuckled softly to himself, pulling through the black rucksack from the back-seat.– He pulled out a black vest t-shirt, unclipped his seatbelt and pulled it over his head, whincing as he did due to the pain it caused him. He then reclipped the belt and leaned back with a sigh of relief.

"Better?" Astrid asked.

He nodded, "Yep I didn't want you overcome with desire at the sight of my half naked form after all." He said with a laugh.

Again, Astrid felt the colour flush in her cheeks, she busied herself checking the mirrors and looking out the driver's side window. "Now you're either going to have to direct me to your place, or put it in the satnav, because my tracking address is limited to the Yellow Pages.

Frank harrumphed well naturedly, and typed in his Seattle address to the satnav. He then leaned back in the car seat and closed his eyes.

Minutes later, Astrid heard the gentle snoring coming from the seat next to her. She turned the radio up, and tried to focus on driving back to Seattle.

2145hrs Frank's Place

Astrid let out an audible sigh as she pulled into the car-lot beside Frank's 34th Avenue address. Her own mobile rang out, she took it from her pocket and answered it.

Her husband David's voice came over the speaker, "Hey Astrid, just checking everything is okay, I expected to see you at home. Its getting late, where are you?"

"I'm fine Dave, just a little tied up here. I got a call out not long after you left, another suspected cyber attack. I'm trying to reboot an entire operating system and reinstall it from scratch." She looked at Frank, and crossed her fingers.

"Are you coming home, or pulling yet another all-nighter?" asked David, he sounded tired, and Astrid could detect the agitation in his voice

"I'm booked into a hotel, I should be home tomorrow afternoon," she replied. "Tell Rachel I'll catch up with her tomorrow night."

""Okay Astrid; I'll see you tomorrow... just, well, be careful." He said, and then hung up before Astrid could reply.

Astrid beat the side of her head with the phone. "For fuck's sake!" Even when she was trying to do something for the greater good, she was left feeling guilty.

Frank looked at her with concern, but chose not to press her. Astrid clearly had a lot going on with her home life.

"Ha'way lassie, get a wriggle on." Frank climbed out from the passenger seat. he slung the rucksack over his shoulder and took the kitbag from the rear seat.

Astrid raised an eyebrow quizzically. As she climbed out she grabbed the laptop bag and followed Frank, assuming that that was what he meant.

They walked towards an apartment block named "The Dakota". The outside was glass fronted with steps leading to the main entrance. Frank led the way, opening the door, dutifully holding it whilst Astrid walked in.

"Thanks," she said, slightly taken aback by his old fashioned manners, then remembered his military background and that he was also clearly a gentleman as well as an Officer.

At the security desk an old slightly balding man sat flicking through the sport section of a newspaper, he had a small portable TV playing a football game with the sound turned all the way down. He looked up and a large smile filled his face.

"Mr McLeod pleased to see you this evening! And this must be....Sarah?" he asked winking at Astrid.

Frank rolled his eyes, "Sorry John, no Sarah, this is a work colleague Michelle... Michelle, John. John, Michelle. Any post for me?"He asked, whilst trying to hide his smile as Astrid tried not to be taken back by the fake name.

"Nope nothing today, and no visitors either. I'll buzz you both up." Replied John pressing the elevator call button from his desk

Astrid and Frank both walked in to the lift car, Frank pressed the button for the tenth floor.

"Have you lived here long?" Astrid asked, trying to mask the nervousness that she felt being in an elevator again with Frank, realising that so much had happened since the last time

"About four years now, pretty much since I took my retirement from the military. It's not bad... quiet. I come and go as I please, someone looks after the communal garden, there's a shared gym, although I have my own equipment in my apartment. But its fine, no one bothers me, it's how I like it. Here we are." Said Frank as the elevator pinged. The doors slowly opened.

They stepped out from the elevator and onto a brightly lit corridor, with parquet flooring and clean fresh white walls. Frank fumbled in the pockets of his combat trousers and drew out a bunch of keys, a keying with an X and the words "I want to believe" dangled from the bunch. Astrid raised an eyebrow.

"Divvint mock, Dana Scully is a thing of beauty... and the series is canny good too." He said with a wink, as he unlocked the apartment door. "Come on in, and make yourself at home."

Astrid walked inside the apartment. The walls were white and crisp. A large 62 - inch flat screen television was mounted flush to the wall, an xBoxOne was connected to the screen, the box for *Call of Duty Infinite Warfare* lay on the white coffee table. One large black leather sofa was placed directly opposite the TV. On the wall opposite hung a canvas abstract painting with slashes of red and blue.

Astrid perched on the right hand side of the sofa, taking in her surroundings

"Come on, we need to take a look at those pages you downloaded. I have a laptop in my bedroom, bring that dodgy copy with ya and we'll have a look, just promise not to look at my browser history." He said with a grin.

Astrid couldn't help but smile, remembering what he had said about his history previously. She followed Frank through a door into his bedroom.

The room was furnished for practicality. A large wooden framed double bed dominated the room, with a black and white striped bedspread, a single pine wardrobe stood in the opposite corner flanked by a pine desk, with a laptop sat in the middle of it. On the walls there were a number of photographs showing the same group of young soldiers, in the middle was a young Frank grinned roguishly at the camera in a variety of poses. Beside the photos there were two framed sets of medals.

Frank booted up the laptop and unlocked the home screen with his password.

"I don't know why I'm hiding this; you'd be able to bust this open in seconds." He said with a laugh.

"Quite likely." She replied.

"Well, I'll let you plug in your do-hickey." He looked pointedly at Astrid's chest. For a few moments Astrid felt herself bristle, till she remembered that she had tucked the memory stick away in her bra. She grinned as she reached inside her bra, pulling out the memory stick. Frank bit his lip, trying not to draw attention to the fact that he had a prime view of Astrid's impressive cleavage.

"Stop perving over the goodies Frank!" she said with a laugh, inserting the drive into the USB port.

The explorer screen opened up and Astrid was able to open the downloaded files. Page after page of photographs from an ornate book, beautifully written in what looked like Latin.

"Sweet Jesus, how many pages are there?" asked Frank in awe.

"We are talking over one hundred here, bloody hell it looks like some kind of ritualistic book." Replied Astrid, flicking through page after page. "In your hidden skills, you don't happen to be able to translate Latin do you?"

Frank chuckled, his warm breath tickled Astrid's neck, sending a soft shiver down her spine.

"No, I can disarm a heavily armed assailant in seconds, but Latin was never one of my strong points. Can we not just use Google Translate?"

Astrid hit her forehead with the palm of her hand, "I know the perfect thing!" she started to tap maniacally on Frank's laptop.

Frank watched awestruck, as Astrid powered through screen after screen, bypassing firewalls, payment screens and typing in random codes until a high-tech version of what looked like the Rosetta stone appeared on his laptop.

"Bloody hell, I could do with you doing that kind of thing with some of my subscription services," He joked. "Seriously though Astrid, how long have you been a computer genius, and why haven't you taken over the world?"

"I cut my teeth on Linux back in 1991, when I was 11, I broke the code and all hell broke out, they paid for my degree and basically allow me to test their new systems to destruction. The majority of operational systems are Linux based, and using that premise I can pretty much get into any network I wish. I am however banned from accessing any FBI related sites," She said with a laugh, "If I do I go straight to jail, do not pass go"

"So how do we go about translating this then?"

"Basically run the program, like this," Astrid replied. "It reckons it will take a few hours to run, at least eight hours looking at the projection."

"Well I don't know about you but I have no desire to sit in front of a computer screen for eight hours. It's Friday night and I could do with some good food and a proper drink I already have the good company. There's a bathroom through there if you want to freshen up. I'll dig out a take away menu."

Astrid walked into the adjoining en-suite bathroom as Frank left the room. It was painted in shades of blue and Division, with nautical décor, Frank had clearly tried to make a feature of the room.

At the side of the sink there lay a cutthroat razor slightly opened beside a shaving brush. A bar of Dove soap sat in the soap dish. On a shelf there were three amber coloured prescription bottles, all made out to Frank McLeod, they were for Valium, Prozac and Temazepam. They had been filed on Monday.

Frank clearly had a lot going on, thought Astrid to herself. Although being ex-SAS, who knew what he had seen, or had been exposed to.

She turned on the taps and washed her face, running her fingers through her hair trying to tease out the tangles. She took off the plaid shirt that she had been wearing and untucked the white tank top from her jeans. She pinched her cheeks to put some colour in them before leaving the bathroom.

Walking back into Frank's bedroom, she checked on the status of the translation program, it was still only two percent complete, she let out a long sigh, this was going to take a while.

Astrid placed her shirt on the chair and took a moment to take a closer look at the medals on Frank's wall. There were a vast number framed indicating tours of Bosnia, Afghanistan and Northern Ireland. In a wooden box frame was a single medal, mounted alone. It hung from a burgundy ribbon, understated, yet the most significant medal of them all, a Victoria Cross. Astrid let out a whistle of appreciation, and then turned to look at the photographs on the wall.

A younger looking Frank, aged around 17 wearing Army fatigues with a group of soldiers all of a similar age, waving their guns above their heads. Given the backdrop, she presumed this was in Iraq.

Another photograph, possibly taken around ten years later, this time Frank was dressed in black fatigues, sporting a moustache. Astrid assumed that he was in his late twenties here. His once wiry frame had now broadened across the shoulders, and the youthful face had the lines of experience just starting to creep in.

She left the room and walked into the living room, Frank had poured out two tumblers of Jack Daniels over ice. He was in the kitchen/diner, on the telephone ordering food from the Chinese judging from the menu on the table.

He hung up the phone, and placed it back on the cradle, he came back into the living room, then sat himself down on the sofa stretching his legs out. He picked up a glass and held it out to Astrid. She stepped forward and took the glass from him. HE then picked up the other glass that had been set next to it.

"Here's to Enigma's greatest fuck up," he said bumping his glass against Astrid's. He took a mouthful of the whiskey. "Christ that's good stuff, I've ordered a banquet for us, I'm just going to change and clean up,I won't be long, food will be around 45 minutes. Make yourself at home."

Frank set the glass back down, and wandered over to his bedroom.

Astrid flicked on the TV and scrolled through the news channels, just in case there were reports of creatures in Seattle. Nothing appeared to be amiss. The President was still fuelling the news with his antics, she leaned back into the sofa, sipping the whisky and watching the reports.

Ten minutes later Frank walked back into the living room, he was wearing a pair of black combat trousers. He was pulling a plain white t-shirt over his head. Astrid could see that he had also changed the dressing on his chest..

"Feel better?" she asked.

Frank nodded. He past by her, heading in the kitchen, where he retrieved the bottle of Jack from the counter. Bringing it back with him into the living room, he refilled his tumbler and topped up Astrid's.

By the time the Chinese had been delivered they had drank half the bottle of Jack Daniels between them, they sat in companionable silence eating the Chinese food until they were both full.

Frank refilled their glasses yet again and watched Astrid as she curled up on the chair, her feet tucked beneath her. Frank noticed how small and tired she looked. He had forgotten that she was new to all this and that she was also in essence only a civilian. Her hair had started to fall out from her functional ponytail, he reached over tucked it back behind her ear, gently cupping her cheek for a moment. In any other situation she would be in his bed.

"Tell me about the medals on the wall in your room" said Astrid, sipping the whiskey and– letting the fire warm her through.

Frank leaned back in the chair and reflected for a moment.

"Well I joined the army at 16, as you probably know from my dossier, I have tours of Bosnia, Iraq, and Northern Ireland. I was in what you would call the regular army until I was 20, then I joined the SAS at 20. I did a several missions whilst there, none of which I can go into detail about. But I served my time. Me, and the boys, well we were rewarded as they saw fit."

"The one on its own, the Victoria Cross, that's kind of a big deal isn't it?"

"It was awarded because I did my job, I keep it as a reminder that despite the shit that went down I did my job, and I did it well."

Frank took another long drink.

"There was this one time we were called out to a hostage situation, around ten years ago, I'll never forget it, there were 19 young women aged from mid teens through to their thirties, they had all been abducted by this weird cult. We found the women in a barn, they had been locked up for about three months, hadn't seen the light of day in all that time. There was gun fire and so much blood. One of the women was so hysterical, I couldn't calm her down. I ended up head-butting her to knock her out just so I could get her outta there. We got all the women out thankfully, the cult members were all killed in the shootout.

Frank looked over to Astrid, who had turned deathly pale, "It's okay lassie, I'm sure that they live quite normal lives now."

"It's not that Frank. Ten years ago I was abducted. I was taken to a barn with 19 other women and we were caged like animals. We were beaten daily, never allowed outside to see daylight. We were terrified, then one day these soldiers dressed head to foot in black burst in through the door, wearing these terrible gas masks, it was terrifying, they started shooting, blood was everywhere, and the screams, oh my God, the screams, they still haunt me. I was picked up by one of them, and he carried me out. I remember the daylight burned my eyes, one of the soldiers head-butted a hysterical woman. Three months without seeing my family. It still haunts me. I can't believe that you were there Frank!"

Astrid wiped the tears from her eyes and regained her composure.

Enigma Division, you crafty bastards, Frank thought.

Frank placed his arm around Astrid awkwardly, and she leaned in towards him.

"You're here now Astrid, and I promise I will do every thing that I can to keep you safe." He kissed the top of her head.

They sat like this for what seemed like hours, each reflecting on how their lives had led them to converge at this point. Strange that a chance encounter had led them to cross paths once more. Was it a chance encounter, or had this all been orchestrated?

06:00 the following day

The computer beeping woke Astrid. She opened her eyes and rubbed the sleep from them, her head ached. Too much Jack Daniels the previous night. She could hear Frank's snoring coming from the living room. She was in the bedroom, but she could recall how she got there.

Astrid yawned and stretched. She rolled herself into a seated position, before cautiously standing up, she walked over to the laptop and checked the status. 100 percent complete translation. She sat at the desk and opened the translation file.

Page after page had been translated, detailing how to perform a resurrection spell to bring a loved one back from the dead. Words and instructions filled each page, sacred beings mentioned within the pages. Spiritual entities from a higher plain. The same name mentioned in several places; Azathoth and *The Other*.

Astrid flicked through the pages on the laptop, again *The Other* was mentioned.

She brought her hand to her mouth in shock as she read through the translation. *The Other* was described as a malevolent spirit or creature which when invoked could possess the dead, the infirm and the dying. It retained memories from those that it possessed and used these to warp and twist the world around in order to reach its own goal, that being to control and destroy all that is sacred and loved. An entity of terror that existed purely to rip apart and destroy lives. Once it had used the host body to its fullest capacity *The Other* would then transfer to another host, again taking the knowledge gained from the previous host and transferring to the new one.

Astrid read further down the pages, *The Other* could only be banished from the body by the use of fire, where it would dissipate and return to what is believed to be its original form and plain.

A cough from the doorway made Astrid jump in fright. She turned to see Frank raking his hand through his tousled hair.

"Frank, you need to read this," said Astrid, standing up and offering him the chair.

He sat in front of the computer screen, and rubbed his eyes, he took a few moments to read through the pages, taking in the information about *The Other*. Astrid looked on in silence, she re-read the contents over his shoulder. Ten minutes later he turned to face her. He too looked visibly shaken.

"Okay, now we know what we are dealing with, and more importantly, we know how to destroy it. Let's get this done."

He stood up and walked to the bed, he reached underneath and pulled out a drawer, it contained body armour, and ballistic chest plates. He took them out and passed one to Astrid, she looked at it with confusion.

"If she hits you like she did me I won't forgive myself, fasten it up as tight as you can."

Frank fastened the armour to his body, he reached back into the drawer, and pulled out a box of bullets, he held his hand out for the Walther PPK, Astrid passed it over to him and watched as he loaded the clip. He put the safety on and handed it back to Astrid.

"If we get through this, I'm teaching you how to shoot. Not if, *when*." He said with a note of determination.

Astrid noticed a look cross Frank's face, he looked harder and more determined. He actually looked quite menacing. He met her eye and flashed a smile.

"Come on Baxter, let's go."

Baughman's Apartment

They returned to New Newbiggin, a sense of urgency and trepidation consumed both Astrid and Frank for they both knew that this was their final chance to undo the damage that they had inadvertently done.

They climbed out from the Land Rover. As Astrid looked at Frank, fear prickled at her skin.

"I don't suppose that you have a handy flamethrower in the back do you Frank?"

"Nope, however I have something just as good, if not better." He reached into the back of the Land Rover and pulled out a brown paper bag, he looked around and pulled the contents up to show Astrid. It was a large bottle of Jack Daniels.

"I was going to save this one for a rainy day, but it looks like today may be that day. I figure we stuff the neck with a rag, light it up and blow her to kingdom come."

Astrid nodded in reply, the reality of what was about to happen became even more apparent.

Frank reached into the first aid kit and grabbed a roll of bandages and a Zippo lighter, he then shoved them in the pocket of his combat trousers.

"Come on, let's check the outside area first."

They walked over to the apartment block, firstly checking closely in the alleyways. The dumpster at the side of the block caught Frank's eye. He turned to Astrid and pressed his finger to his mouth, indicating silence. He motioned to the body between the bins. It looked motionless, but they could not be certain.

Frank glanced around on the ground, and found a broken piece of brick, he picked it up and threw it at the bin. A loud clanging echo filled the alleyway.

The body didn't move.

Frank unholstered his gun, and moved cautiously towards the body, he signalled that Astrid wait at the entrance of the alleyway.

The closer he moved, the more pungent the smell that surrounded the body; the sweet, putrid smell of rotting flesh. Blow flies cascaded and covered the body, a hive of buzzing activity, hundreds of maggots spilled out from her mouth and eye sockets.

Frank gagged, having to cover his mouth with the back of his hand, he turned away.

"She's gone Astrid! We're looking for a new host now, one that's *not* falling apart."

"She must be trying to get back to the apartment. If she comes into contact with Clyde's family. Oh GodFrank, We need to stop her."

"We'll stop her Astrid, you, me and Jack. You owe me a large bottle after this."

Once again they made their way to the apartment block, its dingy interior once again filling Astrid with a sense of foreboding. Only this time, the drunken Hobo was nowhere to be found. For a moment she considered if this was the current host.

"Can we take the stairs this time?" asked Astrid

"You okay lassie?" asked Frank, with genuine concern in his voice, "I'm sorry it's not exactly been easy for you."

"I'm fine Frank, really... Not quite what I expected, it's just the elevator, and it creeps me out. I don't know, it's old and rickety. I just feel happier using the stairwell."

Frank nodded, "Okay, maybe not such a bad idea. We don't wanna get cornered anyhow! Five floors mind. Do you still have the gun I gave you?"

Astrid patted her jeans pocket. Frank noted the tell tale bulge in her pocket. "Okay, let's do this."

Slowly they opened the stairwell door, it was empty, slightly darker, and a light bulb flickered every now and then as the filament gradually burned out.

Astrid could feel her heart pounding in her chest, her breathing became harder and shallower, and she reached into her jacket pocket and pulled out a blue Salbutamol inhaler. She exhaled, shook the inhaler; and then inhaled two doses of the Salbutamol. She coughed as the steroid hit the back of her throat. She instantly felt the benefits of its use, the renewed ability to breath easier.

Frank glanced back with a quizzical look, to make sure she was okay before heading upstairs. As they reached the third floor they both stopped a moment to catch their breath, bracing themselves for the shitstorm that was about to erupt above them.

The corridor was quiet, just like it had been yesterday – this apartment was clearly a hub of activity.

"So what's the plan then?" asked Frank.

"Me? Why are you asking me? You're the Spec Ops Yoda!" Astrid replied in shock.

When she eventually realised that Frank was merely giving her the opportunity to shine, she relented. "Um, I suggest we work our way down the corridor, if we find her, she's sure to react."

"Okay then, but you had better have a good cover story for us." He replied

"Always Frank, always." Astrid said, matter-of-factly.

Astrid walked to the first door. She rapped her knuckle on the blue upvc door, a young woman in her early twenties answered with a baby crying on her hip. She looked both tired and harassed.

"Yeah, who are you?" she asked with a sigh.

"I'm sorry to bother you," began Astrid. "I'm new in the area and my cat's escaped, you haven't seen one in the area have you, a black tabby?"

"No, I'm sorry," replied the young woman. "Animal control are pretty busy around here, have you tried contacting them."

There was a crash in the apartment, followed by the sound of a wailing child, the baby in her arms felt it needed to get in on the act and bellowed even louder.

"I'm sorry, I have to go."

Astrid smiled sympathetically as the young woman closed the door.

"One down, four to go." Said Frank.

They walked to the next apartment; Astrid looked at Frank, who nodded at the door.

"Your turn" she mouthed at Frank.

Frank's eyes crinkled at the corners as he smiled, he knocked on the door, and then pulled a serious face. An elderly man answered the door.

"Good morning sir, can I speak to you about our Lord and Saviour Jesus Christ…" began Frank.

The old man's face broke into a genuine smile, "Well of course, please do come in, I'll put the kettle on."

Frank glanced over to Astrid, a look of helplessness on his face. Astrid bit her cheeks trying desperately trying not to laugh at the predicament that Frank had managed to get himself into. The old boy's response was not what he was expecting.

After fifteen minutes of chatting to the lovely but lonely gentleman, Mr Phillipson, Frank finally managed to excuse both he and Astrid with the promise that they would call back next week. The door closed and Astrid looked over to Frank.

"I don't think that it was him. Perhaps we had better try Mrs Janowitz, because I'm sure that she will be out soon anyway; she was rather nosy."

Astrid walked over the apartment opposite Baughman's. She knocked on the door with a slight prickle of unease at the back of her neck.

A voice came from the other side of the door, "Just a minute..." it sounded older than she did when they exchanged words in the corridor the previous day., She also sounded detached and distracted.

Astrid shot Frank a look, as she took the Walther PPK from her pocket. She dropped her arm to her side so her jacket concealed her small gun from view. Frank took his gun from his holster and mirrored Astrid's actions, concealing his gun with his jacket. After what felt like an age, Mrs Janowitz eventually opened the front door.

She looked unkempt and ruffled, somewhat different from the little old gossiping woman from yesterday, was it really only yesterday?

"Hello, can I help?" she said, a slight look of confusion on her face.

"Mrs Janowitz, how are you? We met yesterday; I wonder if we could trouble you for a spot of tea. We'd like to know a little more about your neighbour…"

Recognition crossed Mrs Janowitz's face, and she opened the door further.

"Of course, do come in." she shuffled to one side; her movements were slow, slightly jerky, not as fluid as before.

Astrid walked into the apartment, it was filled with vintage orange pine, doilies on every surface, little china dogs and photographs of yet more dogs. Astrid glanced around looking for the little Bichon Frise, of which there was no sign. Mrs Janowitz closed the door.

"I'll put the kettle on," she said – walking towards the kitchen.

Astrid watched the old woman walk across towards the kitchen, her eye caught sight of a little white nose at the kitchen door, at first glance it was possible to mistake the dog to be asleep, but there was a tiny pool of what looked like blood that had oozed from the nostrils.
Astrid looked at Frank fleetingly, looked back at the little old woman, and raised the concealed gun.

"Get down on the floor, with your hands above your head." She said evenly.

Mrs Janowitz' mouth formed an "oh" of surprise. "What are you doing? What do you want?"

"Get down on the floor." Demanded Astrid, pulling back the hammer on her gun.

Frank gently placed his hand on Astrid's right shoulder.

"Astrid, think about what you are doing, she's just a little old woman."

"A little old woman, I think not." Began Astrid.

Mrs Janowitz collapsed into a heap on the floor, keening and crying, terrified sobs wracked through her body causing it to convulce.

"That's no old woman Frank," continued Astrid. "She killed the fucking dog... You can see it there in the doorway, now bloody help me!"

Mrs Janowitz continued to keen. Frank was torn between wanting to believe Astrid and that unsettling feeling that she was on the verge of making a fatal error, or at the very least terrifying a little old woman.

The keening continued from Mrs Janowitz, and then she looked up and met Astrid's eyes. The old woman's eyes had a golden tinge that radiated from deep inside. Astrid felt her heart race, as she supported her gun with her other hand in order to stop it from shaking.

"You wouldn't hurt and old woman would you?" began Mrs Janowitz, her eyes narrowed as she took in Astrid's stance. "No, you wouldn't, you're a mother, you wouldn't hurt me, that takes away who you are, who you wish you were. We both know you aren't what they see yourself to be though. You hide Astrid don't you? You bury yourself in that bottle, you know which one, and it's in your desk. Your failure; it taints you. That guilt; – that you let them take you, and allowed them to do all those things to you, you even liked it after a while didn't you? I can teach you things, I can show you how they picked *you* and why they took *you*... Let me... Let me in Astrid, inside your head."

Mrs Janowitz words whirled through Astrid's head, coaxing her, edging her closer to relenting.

"Astrid! Don't listen... keep the gun on her!" Frank's Scottish burr broke through Astrid's trance.

Astrid's expression hardened, she raised the gun again, Mrs Janowitz spat out in fury, she then turned her focus over to Frank.

"I can help you Frank. I know why you cry out in your sleep. I can tell you why she did it, I can bring her back, you and I, we can do it together. We can bring your wife and daughter back,join me, I can show you..."

Astrid shot a glance over at Frank. He had silent tears of pain in his eyes, reminiscing. He looked broken. Astrid swallowed painfully, he had never mentioned a family, his dossier made no mention of one, and as a result she had never asked.

"Frank, Frank she's lying to you. She *can't* help you. She's a monster. Whatever happened, she can't help, what's done is done... please Frank, listen to me!" begged Astrid, desperation filled her voice. "Please listen to me, she can't help. I know you're in pain, but please don't listen to her."

Frank blinked and seemed to shake himself from the trance that he had been under. He looked at Astrid, then back towards Mrs Janowitz, or whatever the monster was that she had become.

"Frank?" began Astrid, watching him closely.

"I can help you Frank..." said Mrs Janowitz.

Frank glanced at the old woman. He tucked his pistol under his arm, with both hands free he reached his left hand reached into his combat trousers pocket, he pulled out the brown paper bag. He also took out a Zippo lighter.

"Astrid, when I tell you to move, fucking do it." He muttered.

Frank opened the bottle of Jack Daniels with his mouth, he spat the lid to the floor. Then using his teeth he pulled out the soaked bandage that had been stuffed into the neck of the bottle. Then he flicked open the Zippo, ignited it, and put it the bottle.

"Astrid, fucking run!" he bellowed, throwing the lit bottle at Mrs Janowitz' feet.

Astrid ran to the door, looking back and screaming Frank's name. The bottle smashed as it hit the floor, the liquor vapourised, immediately ignited and creating a fireball that engulfed Mrs Janowitz. Her shrieks filled the apartment, her body dropped to the floor. A Division hazy apparition appeared seemed to shriek out, and then dissipate.

"Frank!" yelled Astrid, grabbing his arm and pulling him back out towards the apartment door as the fire began to rapidly spread, licking across the floor, and rolling across the ceiling, igniting the old pine furniture that went up like old tinder. They tried to slam the door shut, but the flames poured through.

"Fire, fire!" yelled Astrid banging on the apartment doors, one after another after another.

Frank smashed the fire alarm with his elbow, the sprinklers and fire alarm raged. The sound bounced throughout the apartment block. Doors opened and terrified people emerged from their apartments. Astrid saw the young mother and two terrified screaming children.

"Stairs! Quickly, come on!" Astrid indicated to the mother.

Astrid grabbed the toddler who was screaming like a banshee, Frank grabbed the smaller child.

"Is everyone out?" he demanded of the mother

"I think so… we need to get out, the children!"

They raced down the three flights of stairs, coughing and choking against the acrid smoke that burned against their eyes, and caused tears to stream down their faces. It felt like it took an eternity to reach the bottom of the stairs. They burst out into the lobby.

Astrid's lungs felt as though they would burst as they reached the outside, clean fresh air hit Astrid's lungs making her cough and wheeze. She and Frank carried the children across the road to safety, reuniting the sobbing babies with their mother who had made her own way out, she held them close, showering them with kisses.

"Thank you." She mouthed over their heads at Frank and Astrid.

The apartment block had been completely engulfed in flames, it raged from floor to floor, rapidly consuming the entire building. The parkland that they stood on was filled with people of all ages, crying; terrified, as they watched their homes burn.

The sound of the fire brigades siren echoed around the park as the fire engines pulled up. The Seattle Fire Department quickly got to work; Firefighters carrying equipment and wearing breathing apparatus ran into the building whilst others readied ladders and hoses for their use to fight the flames. The tower block was done for, but at least they could prevent the spread of the flames to adjoining blocks.

The flames licked up the tower block, acrid smoke filled the air, along with the heartbroken sobs and cries of those around Astrid and Frank. The heat from the burning building was so intense, that Astrid felt the sweat pouring down her face. She stood watching the tower as windows began failing, and flames emerged at every level. A wave after wave of sorrow filled her, those poor people, their homes, heirlooms, and everything that had worked for; destroyed and lost forever. And she and Frank were responsible.

"Astrid, don't you fucking dare." The voice whispered in her ear. "Thanks to you these people live another day, thanks to you those kids still have their mother. Enigma will clean up, and they will be fine. Hell, they will probably end up in a better position than they are now. If you dare fucking cry about it, I will personally spank you till I can't lift my arm, and believe me I can go all day and all night. You saved them, actually we *both* did."

Astrid's hand found Franks, and she linked her fingers through his. Frank looked down at their intertwined fingers, then back at her, he smiled, a genuine smile that crinkled his eyes at the corners.

"You did well Baxter, for a newbie, you did well. Now let's get to that Post Office and lay this damn thing to rest.."

The pair walked away from the scene of the fire which continued to ravage the tower block, towards the car lot.

It watched them leave, from deep within the shadows. Hatred oozed from its very presence. The woman... she posed a problem; all eyes must remain on her, she must be stopped, as soon as possible.

The drive towards the Post Office was uneventful. Astrid stank – there was no other word for it, she pulled the sun visor down and looked at her reflection in the mirror. She looked exhausted; she felt it too.

Two days ago, she would never have even imagined that this could or would have happened. She flicked on the radio, Annie Lennox' dulcet tones singing "Sweet Dreams" filled the car.

Astrid smiled as her thoughts immediately travelled to the grumpy Scotsman. He had literally saved several times these past two days, and for this she was eternally grateful.

He had a draw to him, Astrid couldn't deny it; his rugged, sarcastic and grumpy demeanor hid the soul of someone who had been deeply wounded – perhaps not physically but mentally.

They were bound now, like it or not.

The handler watched it all play out.

Enigma had eyes and ears everywhere.

The iPhones provided to them had been calibrated with tracking and recording systems, technology that was virtually undetectable.

The link between Astrid and Frank, that he was part of the team that her from the hostage situation, now this hadn't been identified, someone was definitely going to pay the price for not providing the Intel on this. As it stood, agents were being drafted in to pursue the link and analyse how best to exploit this to the betterment of Enigma.

The woman: Baxter, she had potential, however she also had a rebellious streak, downloading case related materials, this was usually a direct route to instant dismissal! The handler toyed with the idea of having her eliminated, however, she had skills,hidden skills and talents just waiting to be utilised and exploited.

The handler removed his hand from the phone. She had one last chance. He was intrigued, and he wanted to see how this would pan out...

13:05 The Post Office

Frank drove them into the car lot, the same one that she had pulled into yesterday morning. It felt like a lifetime ago, and to all intents and purposes it was.

She climbed out from the car and her eyes met the Division eyes of Frank's. She ran to the Land Rover and took the laptop case as Frank dragged out the kitbag.

"Come on, almost there."

They walked into the Post Office together, towards the counter. The old, balding gentleman from yesterday was sitting working through a soduku puzzle. He glanced up from his newspaper and his face broke into a genuine smile. Astrid doubted if he had actually moved from that spot since yesterday.

"Good afternoon, what a pleasure to have you back!"

Frank rolled his eyes. "I'd like to send a couple of packages if possible. Special delivery, it needs to be tracked."

Frank placed the kitbag on the counter, Astrid placed the laptop in its bag on top. Frank looked pointedly at the teller.

"I assume that all details have been completed… and necessary paperwork included?" Responded the teller, not batting an eyelid.

"Yep, all present and correct. To be sent and dealt with as a priority."

The teller took the packages, and handed a clip board over to Frank in order to sign for the consignment.

"If you wouldn't mind signing, then we can arrange payment for services rendered. Rest assured, your support and efforts have been appreciated in this endeavour, you shall be rewarded accordingly. Sign below the x's please."

As Astrid scrawled her signature beneath the x she was unable to hide the feeling that this meant so much more. Was this the end, or simply the beginning?

"Check your accounts tonight, details have been sent to your email. We would like to thank you for your continued support." The teller concluded.

Astrid and Frank walked out from the Post Office in companionable silence. As they reached the carlot, Astrid stopped and grabbed Frank's hand, her palm was slick with sweat from nerves, adrenaline and everything else.

"Is that it?" she asked.

Frank smiled, "It never is Astrid, not with Enigma, they will call when they need you, always on their terms. You don't find them, they *will* find you."

He reached over and pushed a loose tendril of hair behind her ear again. Their eyes met, and Astrid felt the bubbles rise in her stomach. Frank towered over her, and he gently kissed her forehead.

"Astrid Baxter, it's been a goddamn fucking pleasure, in more ways than one."

Astrid opened her eyes after the kiss, she glanced up, and met Frank's eyes, acutely aware of his hand in the small of her back; she knew that here and now was the defining moment in their fledgling relationship.

And though she wanted to see where it could lead, with every fibre in her body, she chose not to.

"Next time Frank... or, preferably *before* next time, teach me to shoot."

Frank grinned, hiding the fact that he too knew what had just passed between them. "Baxter, it would be my pleasure. Come to the range next week, I'll teach you."

As they reached their cars Frank stopped. He looked down at Astrid once more, her hair was a mess, she stank of smoke, her jeans were stained with Christ only knew what. She looked like a lost soul. He took her in his arms and held her closely, she sank against the hard leanness of his body. Her fingers curled through the hair at the nape of his neck.

For the first time in almost ten years, Frank felt his resolve weaken. He caught her wrist in his hand, lifted it to his face and kissed the inside of her wrist.

"Astrid... I will follow you to the ends of the earth. I will protect you and your family. I promise you." He released her hand and walked to the Land Rover. He climbed in, started the engine, and drove away.

19:00 Home

It was dark, outside. The fire was blazing, warming the house, Astrid was sipping Jack Daniels from a tumbler, freshly showered, cuts and bruises tended to, clothing worn to cover the injuries, watching the news.

"Did you hear about the fire at the apartment mom?" asked Rachel sitting beside Astrid.

"It sounds terrible," said Astrid, guardedly.

"Those poor people, no homes left." Said Rachel sadly.

Astrid held her close, and kissed her cheek.

"At least they got out alive sweetheart." She murmured.

The news switched to a report about the fire, the reported stood a safe distance from the remnants of the scene.

"Reports are unable to identify the cause although it is believed that it started on the third floor of the apartment block. Thanks to some quick actions, the block was evacuated with only two casualties; Mrs Edna Janowitz aged 67 and Mr Paul Phillipson aged 84…"

Astrid dropped the glass, it shattered on the floor.

"Mom, mom are you okay?" asked Rachel, fear and concern in her voice as she watched the colour drain from her mothers face.

"I'm fine, I'll clear this up." Replied Astrid, as she picked up the shards of glass and walked into the kitchen, she dropped them in the bin and sat down at the dining table.

She broke down, into uncontrollable tears, her body shook as she buried her head in her hands.

Her husband looked helplessly confused at Rachel. He had no idea what was going on, he had found smoke damaged clothing in the trash can outside. Now wasn't the time to press, but questions needed to be answered?

He brushed his finger tips against the business card in his trouser pocket, he only hoped that the Private Investigator he had hired would have something worth reporting, and soon.

Frank's Apartment

The light shined in Frank's bedroom. He is sat on the bed, his footlockerlay opened on the bed beside him. A photo album is on his knees, a wedding photograph, a younger Frank aged twenty-three, dressed in his full dress uniform, short hair, clean shaven, with a beautiful redhead in his arms, his cap on her head, the train from her wedding dress draped over his arm, both smiling at the camera, full of promise and joy. His bride, Sophie.

Another photograph, this one showing Frank, Sophie and a tiny baby girl taken five years after the first photograph. Again, love shines on their faces, hope and joy for what the future has to hold.

Frank takes a long drink from the bottle of Jack Daniels, not the one Strid owed him, but onther he procured on his way home., He wasn't bothering with a glass, but instead drank straight from the bottle. He opens a note, the one that Sophie left.

'Frank, I'm sorry. I just can't do it anymore.

You aren't here, and neither is she. I can't do this, I love you but I hate you, you left me and you left her, you left me when I needed you the most, and now she's gone, I can't do this anymore."

Her body was found a day later, three days after their daughter had passed away.

He breaks into sobs that wrack through his body.

In the shadows, it watches. Closely.

Feeding from the despair.

Time would tell, as it began to weave its web, entwining Frank and Astrid lives, they were bound together, it would see to that, and revenge would be his.

The End…
For now.

About the Author

Ashley Bell is proud to (finally) independently publish, via Amazon Kindle direct her first novel – Last Things Last.

Ashley lives in the North East of England in the picturesque county of Northumberland with her partner Mick, son Mark, pugs Peggy and Shadow, cat Loki and rabbit Picard.

A keen reader and aspiring author Ashley has dreamed of publishing her own novel – and finally she has been brave enough to give it a try.

Note from the author

Dear reader,
(Wow it feels amazing to actually write this!)

Thank you so much for taking the time to read this little novella.

Writing is not just about creating a story or stringing words together – its about creating an experience. Its about transporting the reader to another world, allowing them to see through different perspectives and opening their minds to new possibilities.

Thank you for joining me on this journey and for investing your time and energy on my words.

I hope you enjoy it.

Astrid and Frank will be back.

Love
Ash x

Printed in Great Britain
by Amazon